GW00865896

Mr. Starfis
and the Mystery Skull

Mark J. Towers

1st Edition published in 2022

Copyright © 2022 Mark J. Towers

All rights reserved.

ISBN: 9798357473141

Double, double.
It's All Hallows' Eve.
Is Mr. Starfish in trouble?

Is he even aware
of things in the ocean
who are planning to scare?

Halloween isn't celebrated under the sea.
They don't even have tasty trick or treat candy!

But imagine if they knew what joy could be had
dressed as a scary vampire to frighten Dad.
Or creeping and shouting, "Boo!" behind Mum.
Then fish too could have spooky Halloween fun!

So, get ready to carve out a giant winter squash.
And remember, in the sea things don't go bump.
They go splosh!

Mr. Starfish was collecting sea lettuce to make a nice sea salad. As he gathered the crop, a sea cucumber wiggled past and greeted Mr. Starfish with a cheery, "Hello!"

Does the cucumber in your fridge speak? The ones in the sea do, so this is a good reason not to eat sea cucumber. Another reason is they are very slimy! Yuck!

As he returned home with a basket full of sea lettuce, Mr. Starfish noticed a dark silhouette descending from above.

WHAT COULD IT BE?

"Oh, my golly, that shadow is dark. I hope it's not Justin, the sharp-toothed shark!"

But it wasn't a shark-shaped shadow.

Mr. Starfish watched the shady shape until it disappeared behind a kelp forest.

THUD!

A wave of sand rushed through the kelp, knocking Mr. Starfish off his feet!

"Wow!" exclaimed Mr. Starfish. "That 'thud' I can't ignore. I must see what it is. I must go and explore."

Mr. Starfish and his pet catfish, Terry, crept through the kelp forest in search of the mystery object.

At the edge of the forest, Mr. Starfish stopped and said, "Well, here we are, my friend. We've reached the end, so what did descend? It's time to be brave, though my knees are shaking as I speak. Well, here we go, Terry. It's time to take a peek."

Mr. Starfish parted the kelp and gasped.

WHAT DO YOU THINK IT COULD BE? A SUBMARINE? A GRUMPY SNORKELING CAT? BROCCOLI? NO! SOMETHING MUCH SCARIER!

Whatever it was, Terry wasn't interested. Instead, he gave the nearest kelp a really good sniff.

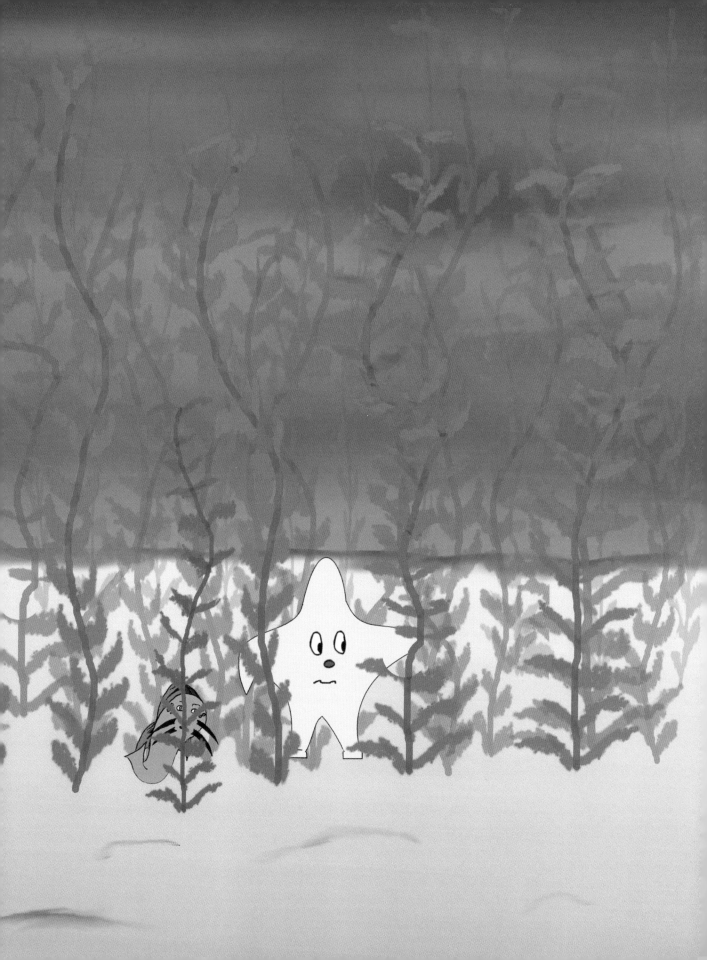

Looming over Mr. Starfish was a giant skull, with an open mouth like a cave entrance.

Mr. Starfish walked over to the skull.

"H...H...Hello? Hello?" said a very scared Mr. Starfish into the skull's open mouth. His words echoed back.

"Ello! Ello! Ello! That's what you sound like!" someone said in a squeaky voice.

Mr. Starfish turned around and was surprised to see an axolotl floating behind him.

"Axel, you startled me as I explore. Do you know how this skull got here on the ocean floor?"

"I don't know," Axel said, "but it's not the only strange thing to land here today! Come with me, Starry, and I'll show you."

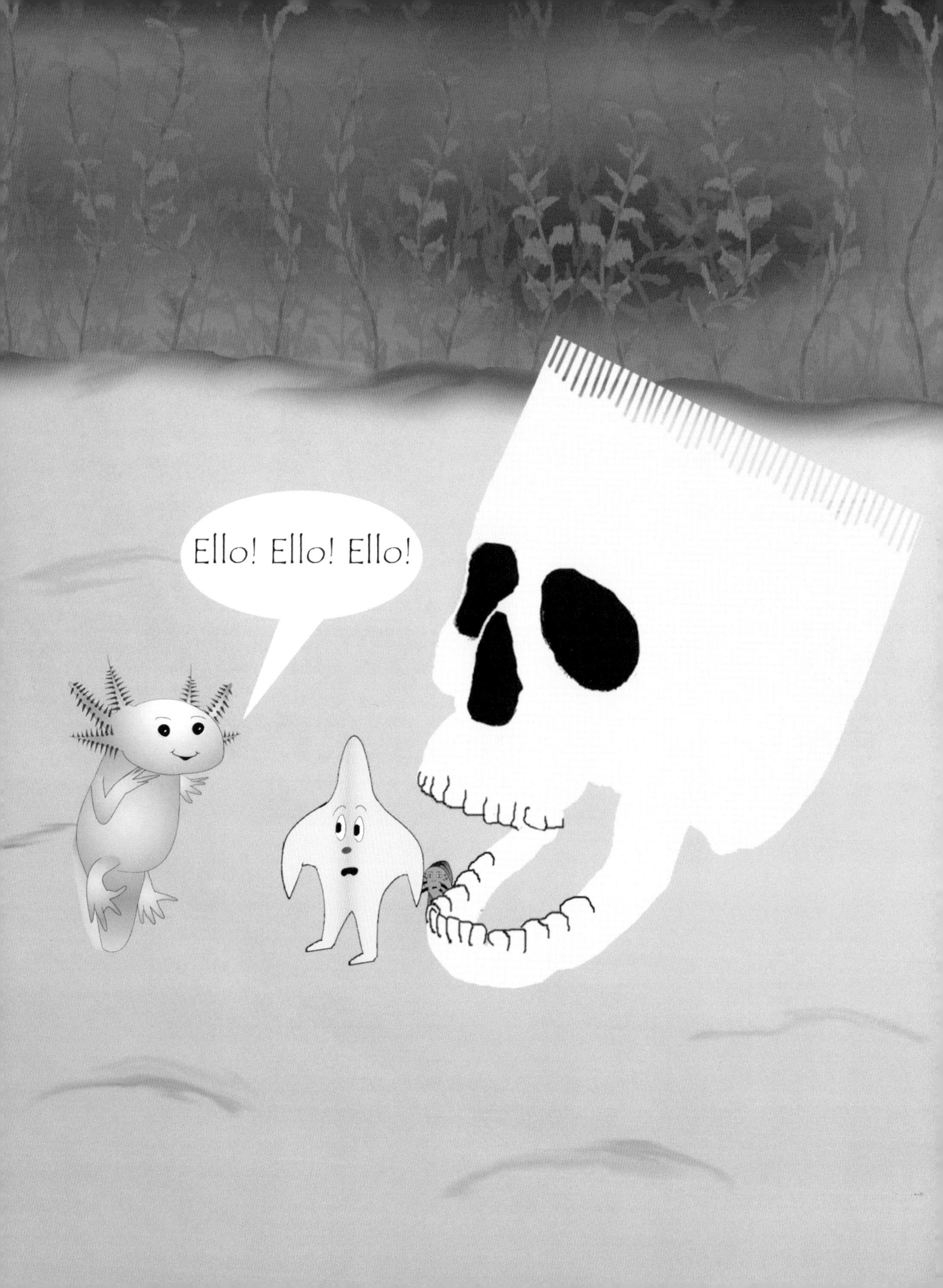
Ello! Ello! Ello!

"Lead the way, and we will follow. Let's go before it gets dark, and today becomes tomorrow!"

"We should take this skull with us," Axel suggested.

"Your idea is good, and I agree in full. But how do we move this giant skull?"

As they pondered this problem, Mr. Starfish noticed it was getting very dark very quickly. Above, another shadowy shape moved towards them.

IF IT WAS ANOTHER SKULL, THEY WOULD BE SQUASHED!

Mr. Starfish and Terry stared. Axel panicked, closed his eyes and ran around in a circle.

The object grew bigger before everything went grey.

Slowly, they opened their eyes.

"**BOO!**" boomed a loud voice.

"**AAARGH!**" screamed Mr. Starfish, Terry, and Axel. They *all* ran around in circles this time. After a few moments, they stopped running and looked up.

There above them was Justin the shark, with a big toothy grin.

"I'll take the skull there for you," said Justin.

"Er, well, maybe. Do you know where *we* are taking it?" Axel asked.

"Oh yes! Near to Hal's cave," said Justin.

Mr. Starfish looked shocked.

"Yikes, Hal the conga eel? The last time I met him, he tried to make me his meal!" Mr. Starfish said.

"Don't worry, my pointy little friend. I'll look after you. Would you like a ride there in my mouth?" Justin asked.

Mr. Starfish and Axel looked at each other. Justin had tried to eat them both before. Several times.

"We'll walk!" said Mr. Starfish and Axel together.

As they arrived near Hal's cave, it was getting dark.

Mr. Starfish switched on a torch and light fell across rows of gravestones. Axel and Mr. Starfish took turns reading some out as they walked through.

"Here lies my sense of humour. Mr. R U Joking."

"I told you something smelt fishy. Ima Kipper."

"This is my final resting plaice! Dolph Fin."

Beyond the gravestones, several strange things stuck out of the sand. Objects Mr. Starfish had never seen before. Orange pumpkins, coffins, a cauldron, a scythe, a witch's broom, and a pointy hat.

Justin decided this was a good place to drop the skull. It landed with another big thud.

This is
my final
resting
plaice!

Dolph Fin

I told you
something
smelt fishy

Ima Kipper

In loving
memory of,
oh I've
forgotten

Colin the
Goldfish

Here lies
my sense
of humour

Mr. R U Joking

Rest
in Pisces

Sue Shi

As the sand cleared, they heard a loud hiss coming from the skull.

OH NO! DOES IT HAVE A PUNCTURE?

"Welcome to the Scare Zone!" the skull hissed.

A face appeared in one of the eye sockets, and Hal the eel slithered out.

"So," Hal hissed. "Do you want a trick or treat?"

Axel looked at Mr. Starfish.Mr. Starfish looked at Axel. Terry sniffed the nearest rock.

Mr. Starfish said, "The question sounds easy...We will have to see. If I say treat, what could it be? A treat would be neat, if it's truly a treat. Perhaps a cake, or a cup of tea. But I'm not sure. What is this trickery?"

Hal's eyes spun around, the same way they did when he hypnotised his dinner.

EEK! SPINNY EYES! IS MR. STARFISH GOING TO BE HAL'S LUNCH?

Then Hal remembered they were guests and not his next meal.

"Trick or treat?" Hal repeated the question. "To be honest, I haven't got a clue what it means. I saw it on a sign."

He pointed to a sign with his tail.

"Here, have one of these. It's my treat to you tonight."

Hal offered them bright red candy-coated apples.

"Er, Hal, what is all this stuff?" said Axel.

"I'm not sure. It fell from up there." Hal gazed towards the sea surface. "It all looks fun, so I decided to gather it all together and throw a party!"

Hal picked up a conch shell with his tail and declared, "Welcome, all sea-dwellers. I'm Hal the eel. It's now evening, so let's have some fun. I declare tonight 'Hal Eel's Eve!'"

Everyone liked the idea of Hal Eel's Eve.

Well, maybe someone, or something, didn't. Just behind them, the cauldron started bubbling and glowing.

OH HADDOCKS! WHAT THE KIPPERS IS GOING ON?

"Hubble bubble! You're all in trouble!" someone cackled.

They all looked up and saw a witch swimming down towards them!

I've never seen a witch swim, but apparently, they're very good at it.

Witches can be scary, so remember these magic words to say just in case you meet one:
"OOOOOH BUGGY BOO! I'M NOT SCARED OF YOU! I'M BIG AND BRAVE, AND YOU SMELL LIKE CABBAGE STEW!"

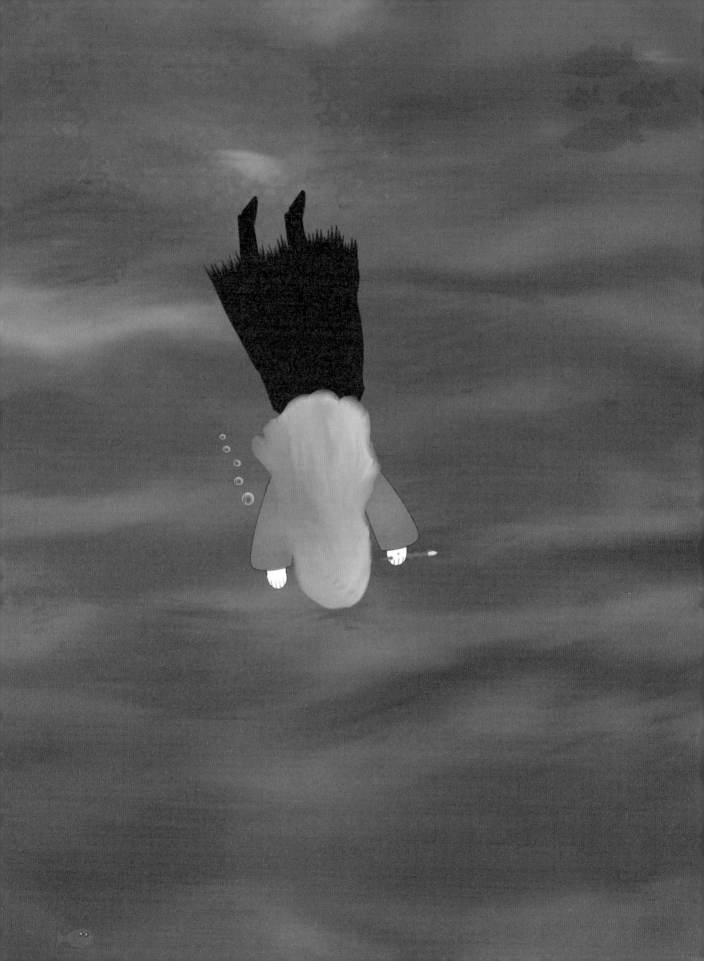

The witch landed on the seafloor, picked up the broom, and put on the pointy hat.

"These are mine," she said, and, looking around, "this is **ALL** mine! I have a good mind to turn you all in to...bats!"

"Sticky round thing on a stick?" said Hal, offering a candy-coated apple, thinking the sweet treat might calm the wicked witch.

"**THEY'RE MINE TOO**," snapped the witch. "Right! That's it." She marched towards the cauldron, muttering something about newts, woolly hats, and hairy wizard's legs.

The witch busied herself at the cauldron, stirring the bubbling pot with her wand.

"You there with the pointy head." She pointed at Mr. Starfish.

"Yes, Mrs. Witch? You asked for me. Please don't cook us. This is my plea."

The witch looked puzzled, possibly because she had never met a rhyming starfish before.

"Fetch me some blind worm's sting!"

"Sorry, Mrs. Witch, I don't know what that is. The only thing I have is this." He offered her some sea lettuce.

The witch grabbed it and took a small bite.

"IT'S FANTASTIC!" she screamed, then tossed it in the cauldron, chanting, "Double, double, toil and trouble..." over and over.

"I'm pleased you enjoyed it, and I don't want to make a fuss, but dare I ask what you're going to do to us?" Mr. Starfish asked.

Do you know what the wicked witch did? She made them watch cartoons and eat humongous ice cream sundaes until their bellies were full. Oh, the horror!

THE END.

Only kidding!
She gave her wand a wiggle and a wave...

ZZZZZZAAAAAP!

The wave of the witch's wand magically gave everyone a spooky costume.

Mr. Starfish now looked like a pumpkin, Axel was a scary monster, Terry had a vampire cloak and fangs, and Justin was wearing a ghostly bed sheet with a ball and chain on his tail fin.

And Hal? Hal was now a toad! An *actual* slimy toad!

"Oh my, what was that? This day is getting strange. From lettuce picking to a giant skull, and now this outfit change. I hope this is the end to an unusual pattern. Surely nothing else odd could actually happen?" Mr. Starfish said.

"Enough of the rhyming, Starry. Witch, why did you do this to us?" Axel asked.

The witch cackled. "It's All Hallows' Eve...Halloween!"

"This might be a dumb question, a sort of a query," Mr. Starfish started, "but, what does that mean? Because it sounds rather eerie!"

"It's time to party!" said the witch.

The witch waved her wand again and began wiggling her botty. Music started playing and disco lights shone from the seabed.

Ghosts and skeletons started dancing.

Fish started dancing.

One little starfish boogied too.

Hal's Halloween wordsearch

Candy
Cauldron
Ghost
Halloween
Pumpkin
Scary
Skeleton
Skull
Spooky
Treat
Trick
Witch

N	E	E	W	O	L	L	A	H	H
J	I	S	Y	R	C	Z	I	C	N
F	N	K	U	R	H	A	T		
M	O	E	P	Z	A	I	N		
K	R	L	D	M	W	C	C	D	B
C	D	E	S	J	U	T	S	B	Y
I	L	T	L	I	A	P	U	U	H
R	U	O	A	E	G	H	O	S	T
T	A	N	R	S	P	O	O	K	Y
X	C	T	L	L	U	K	S	B	S

Witch's sum spell - A tricky treat!

Add the items up to work out the answers. The first one is done as an example. Can you make your own tricky picture sums?

=1 =3 =2 =4

+ + = 9

+ + =

+ + =

Spot the difference

A spell has gone wrong! Can you spot the 8 differences on the Witch?

Colour in Mr. Starfish!

Books by the author

Mr. Starfish series

The Christmas Starfish

Mr. Starfish and the Mystery Skull

Picture Books

Strawberry Scoreberries

I Wish It Were Raining

All books available at Amazon

Visit the author's website: marktowers.co.uk

Printed in Great Britain
by Amazon

87749244R00027